Tears
of
Me

VMH Publishing
Atlanta

Tears of Me

LaToya Martin

As a teen, I had more of a love for drawing instead - writing was never interesting to me. In school, I had a particular assignment and that's when I wrote my first poem called "What Love is Like." A lot of my classmates liked the poem and in that moment, I thought, I may be good at this. Years later as many trials in my life began to unfold, I began writing more and more, and overtime my love for poetry grew. It became an outlet for me to be able to release all the emotions I was feeling.

Writing poetry has helped me cope with a tremendous amount of hurt and pain, and it has also helped me to express myself more. It's always my desire to convey positive messages to my readers. It is my goal to teach and spread God's Word through my poetry, so that people who stumble upon my work may find comfort and healing. There is power in words. I want people to be able to view my work and say, "She understands how I feel!" I believe my poems are rays of light, and so my poetry is a reflection of me.

-LaToya Martin

John Doe

Why have you chosen me?
Why am I considered your best friend?
Why do you see your happiness in my future?
Daily, I receive your many gifts
Oh, how thoughtless are you
Your smile doesn't bring me joy
When I wake up you are there
Silently holding my hand
Preparing to lead me into my day
As the night approaches
You comfort me
You are always included in my prayers
Even though you are strongly against them
Why have you chosen me?
Where did you come from?
Your many words are silent
But yet you are well heard
You will not accompany me in my future
But I must acknowledge that you were a part of
my past
You once departed so why did you return?
How dare you invite yourself back into my life!
Do you not respect my wishes?
You are no longer welcome here
Because my will is to live
So goodbye, cancer

Weed in the Garden

Gardener, why was I planted here?
What did you see?
The gardener replied, a little weed from the earth
standing with nobody
But the sun burns, said the weed
When the rain pours, it hurts
At times I am buried and feel unwanted by the dirt
Don't you see I'm weak?
Many thoughts but can barely speak
Oh, gardener, I beg you, please release me
I'm not clothed in beauty or appealing to see
Wait! Don't walk on by
Don't you see my pain?
No strength, no roots, much loss, much shame
All I ask is that you release thee
So I can stand with the weeds
Who once stood by me
The gardener replied,
Oh, little weed
So well-spoken yet quite demanding
I will not release thee because
You are withered and burned
But yet still standing

"You can overcome depression."

Walketh Out of Heaven

We have an unconditional love
That mends us faithfully and true
Into the mirror, I see that
I am a reflection of you
I asked God for someone special
And my father sent me you
He made a wise decision
Because to you, I'll say I do
We'll remain married
Till death do us part
But we'll reunite in Heaven as angels
Singing gospel from our hearts
You are my love
Even more, my best friend
Like alpha and omega
You are my beginning and my end
I can't tell you how much I love you
As this paper catch my tears
But you are that high mountain peak
That I climb without facing fear
When I see you smile
You open Heaven's gates
All I see is love
And never a sign of hate
I don't know if you are human
Or an angel sent from above
But I know you are my husband
So beautiful like God's love
You bring me strength, love, and joy
You are my voice when I pray

You are my special gift from Heaven
That I unwrap every day

That Archaic Tree

Standing there lifeless
Beaten by time
Birds are no longer attracted to thee
Roots are no longer its backbone
Wishing the leaves would cover it
But they have fallen and withered away
That fragile tree
The rain has ignored him
Forsaken by the sun
An outcast to the wilderness
Waiting for its help to come
Help, that it once provided shade for
Standing there lifeless
Still waiting for a return
That lonely, abandoned, tired tree
Our elders

Eye Concealer

A gift given in advance
To hide the lies within me
Prepared for many nights
Secured for many mornings
Calm and caring
A distraction that's willing to please me
True to my ignorance as it unfolds
Please never leave me
Hide the man that I love
Continue to uphold my marriage
Eye concealer, covering me from yesterday's
mistake
And has prepared me for tomorrow's also
Your many cures erase blank stares
You were once the shade my mother wore
Blending away self-help, pain and anger
You are my beauty routine
Trustworthy and free
A shield for his weakness
But has blended away me

Someone Was Praying For Me

My car accident, my seat
Was thrown many feet, I did not leave
My breath saved by the words
That no one can defeat, prayers lifted me
Someone was praying for me
I was badly beat by the fist
That once said we would forever be
The bruised bones in my body were broken
Many people saw, but when asked they didn't see
Someone was praying for me
When I homeless on the streets
No shoes, no clothes, no home to rest my feet
No warmth, no love from known hearts that beat
But someone was praying for me
I was lost, full of shame
And burned by the heat
Wounded and laughed at by tongues who hated me
Minds of tissue wanted me to sink
Below the dirt where only the dead rest their feet
Your mindless thoughts shall never speak
Because someone is always praying for me

My First Love

From the ocean's first gallon of water
The first flake of snow
Your love carried me
My heart you held so close
From the first spoken word
From when the first footprint was drawn
Your love carried me
Strong from dusk until dawn
From the first child's birth
The first thought of man
Your love carried me
Deep, gripped, firmly in your hand
From the mouth's first smile
The first sense of touch
Your love carried me
No less but so much
From the first forgiven sin
Your love carried me
Pure, strong, out and in
Your love, his love
Pure and perfect carried me
Jesus, my first love

Rebecca

Sold for what she wasn't created to be
Given for the pleasure of another
Oh how pain is now her newfound love
Beaten by the hands that constantly degrade her
Forced to love those same hands
Wants to give up
But struggles for her children
Oh, dear Rebecca
Thrown away into tomorrow's day
Seeing a future that can't be visible
Oh how she once admired the sun
But now angry at its rays
For it despises her skin
Here today
But wishes she was gone tomorrow
Ready to meet the God
Who left her, she claims
Now hanging from the same tree
Her grandmother once owned
Now a breeze of the field
Finally released and allowed to return home
My dear Rebecca

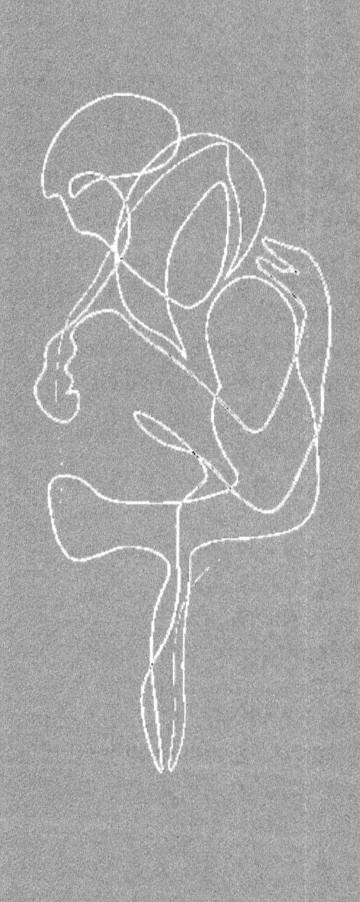

I Miss Him

The hugs I barely gave you
The 'I love you's' I never said
The way my eyes judged you
As your heart secretly bled
My heart a now bottled letter
That has vanished and washed away
Leaving droughts and empty happiness
That will one day return, I pray
I remember the laughs
The pain we shared
The distance, the lack
That was always there
Your memories I now live
A part of me no longer here
A lamb called by our shepherd
On how I miss so dear
The last smile you gave I captured
As I glanced from afar
Wishing to replay that moment
To have and hold you as you are
Lord I miss him
My dear brother

This Christmas

He went on and on about his childhood
About how he walked miles to school barefoot in
snow
Oh how we chuckled to his many stories
Grandpa spoke about where he and grandma first
met
He rambled about life
And how the news was so important to watch
How saving money was mandatory
And material things wasn't
I remember the smell of his homemade biscuits
baking in the morning
Long before the rooster crowed
He attended his garden faithfully as if resting was
a sin
Grandpa's words were heard miles away
Even if he spoke in silence
As a child he didn't have presents for Christmas
So he explained that we should be thankful
Even if nothing was wrapped with a bow and
given as a gift
I remember as he sat in his recliner
And his gray hair shimmered under the lights
And how all of us kids would laugh when he and
grandma argued
This year will be different
Now it's our time to reminiscence about *him*
He has decided to finally rest
Because Grandpa won't be here this Christmas

Dear Life

Why did you abandon me?
Oh, how I barely knew you
Why didn't time defend me?
Why was my last day given permission to
destroy my first?
A young soul I was
Wishing for life
While being destroyed by another
I remembered how your voice echoed
As I listened from within
Oh, how I barely knew you
Not knowing I was someone before I entered
your womb
And never given a chance to be someone after

Friend of the Family

I love you
Yet I hate you
You are the hope of my future
You were my guidance in my past
My father despised you
But my mother adored you
You were her will to live
You were a constant guest in our home
You were the scent my mother wore daily
She neglected me for the happiness of you
She confided in you
But your greed took her away
After all the hurt and pain you caused
I welcomed you back into my life
But now you are my foundation
I finally see what my mother saw in you
You helped her cope with her wounds
Even though you helped cause them
My family doesn't understand you
And honestly nor do I
You've ruined my past
And I have acknowledged
That you have ruined my future
You are the end of my tunnel
My whiskey bottle

A Withered Rose

You have taken the future goals in his life
The colors of his rainbows
His last breath to live
You've stolen the freedom of joy in his veins
The happiness in his smiles
You've interrupted a life of confidence
Low self-esteem has taken his soul
His candles once burned a light of determination
A motivation flame can never ignite
You have taken his inner beauty
And have destroyed the walls of his outer
appearance
You have burned the dreams of a cheerful rose
That is no longer awakened by the sun
For he is withered by the sexual abuse
That was concealed in one man's wicked heart

Forever Heaven

My time
My place, my home
Eternity, my throne
Appreciates my love, my truth
Happiness and joy, never alone
A place where beauty isn't an issue
No competitions, no fame
Just laughter, no rains
No tears, bitterness, no claim
Beautiful, peaceful
No living soul can describe
No hate, no sorrows
No scars to hide
My heart, my joy
No guilt, no shame
Forever and Heaven
My daughters, their names

Grief

My child
Still gone
Lord, where were you?
Why is my breath so important
Was his breath not?
Living is now a curse
My shadow now criticizes its light
Empathy from others I consider pain
Hugs are just a constant duty
Why do I awake?
Why does morning care?
And how night pampers me, but my bed resists
Stress is now my companion
Oh how it comforts me during restful nights
My child
Still gone

Forgive Me, Lord

Forgive me for my unrighteousness ways
Forgive me for not turning my nights to days
Forgive me for the hatred that dwells deep in my
heart
Forgive me for not letting my anger depart
Forgive me for stubbornness that lives in my bones
Forgive me for my wicked mind that leads me on
and on
Forgive me for not acknowledging you, and letting
anger take my inner being
Forgive me for my ungrateful thoughts and
allowing intense doubt to stop my believing
Forgive me for being so distant by rejoicing and
serving your name
Forgive me for blaming you for all of my
weaknesses and pain
Lord, I thank you for forgiving me

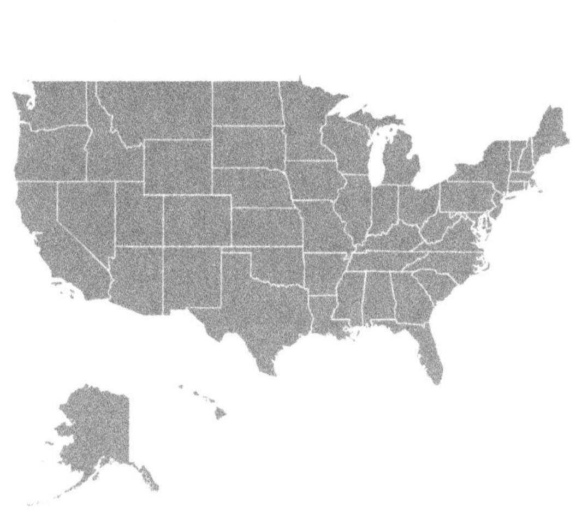

Honored Uniforms

I honor you
I honor the tears in your eyes
Your wounds of broken skin
I honor the weapon that guided you
The weapon many of you carried daily, the Holy
Bible
I honor your confidence, your fear
I honor you as one
One mind, one strength, one fight
More importantly
I honor love
Your love protecting our country

A Father's Way

A father leads
A father loves
His love ascends surpassing beauty in its mold
A father builds, a father molds
His hand - his child's future
His strength - his child's guide
His smiles should encourage
His wisdom should snow
A fathers love not many will know
Father, a word watered but seldom grows

Suicide

43

Beaten by the hands that held me throughout the
night
My self-esteem is low
I can't leave, I can't fight
Beaten by his problems that are taken out on me
My self-esteem is low as he chokes me; I can't
breathe
Beaten by his past that's taken over his mind
My self-esteem is low, my prayers will God ever
find?
Beaten by the alcohol that has taken over his soul
My self-esteem is low, I've pushed myself through
the coals
Beaten by his love
As it forced me to stay
My self-esteem is gone
Now in my grave I lay

Big Momma

Strong, honest, wise
Provided a future for her own
Happy, secure, and brave
But sometimes wishes she was home
Loving, serene, Godly
At times worry overrides
Humbled, cheerful, and kind
At times it runs and hides
Gives advice, rambles about life
Never wrong, always right
Shelters her family through the frigid winds of
the weather
Fading health on a mission to soon get her
Caring, gentle, helpful
Forgetful and strict at times
Hatred, weak, and bitterness - in her you will
never find
Big Momma

Mirror

Blamed for displaying broken images
For ignoring inner beauty
Blamed for awarding the outer mask
A trap for the weak as well as the strong
Mirror, approached for advice
But itself, broken and replaced
Honest, opinion its own
Mute and alone
Mirror, blamed for revealing you
A reflection distracted from its inner core
Pure, non-judgemental, and always for

Your Whisper on My Pillow

Telling me to remember you
Reminding me of our past
Wishing our emotions can once again build
Telling me not to dismiss you
Impelling me to hold on to your memories
Your pillow lying there empty and motionless
Reminding me of what could have been our
future
Then I awakened
Your whisper on my pillow
Suddenly fading

Clueless

When you leave
He's welcomed in your home
He eats your meals, wears your clothes
He loves your wife
Yet you are clueless
When he calls, she exits
She lowers her voice
She speaks to him with her loving words
The same words that have deceived your mind
She leaves and returns
You are up waiting, you ask, she lies
Yet you are clueless
No matter how she hurts you
You welcome her home
Your home where trust has been broken
Broken by the lust of your wife
A wife who questions her love for you

52

Dear My Mother's Pain

I'm sorry for bringing you shame
I'm sorry for calling your name
While suffering and you did not a thing
I'm sorry for my sibling's death
When you left us alone and went out the door
You told me to watch over them
Mom, that's what *you* were for
I forgive you for calling me worthless
And never giving me endless hugs
But when the pride of the streets came
You gave it all of your love
I forgive you for leaving me
And not hiding your feelings from the truth
I'm now gone from this life
And I hope this letter gets to you

-    Your loving child

54

Mary Wept

My son
Your son
Given yet taken
A seed I've nurtured
From the day it was sown
My son, here for a purpose
But also taken for one
Oh how my heart wept
As his journey began
He's yours, I know Lord
But yet still mine
Here for tomorrow
But taken before today
Your son, my son, our son
Jesus

That Restless Day

My heart sank
Its beats were paralyzed
A mother's nightmare
I hear the church bells calling
But I dare not answer
When that day approached
My prayer was offered
But it was refused
A day where God's decision was made
The hours ticking
The minutes vanishing
That day approaching
And finally here
But will continue to return each year
As I remember that day
My brother was called home

-     In Memory of My Brother

58

When the Rain Falls

It doesn't flee
It strains as it flows
It touches what it is given
It wanders
Its growth pursues in time
When the rain falls
It doesn't seek shelter
It doesn't seek guidance
It pursues the highest tree
When the rain falls
It doesn't flee
It strains as it flows
Its growth pursues in time

A Rose's Thorn

Standing and waiting
Alone at times pacing
Petals are plucked
Withered and burned
Mirror reflects ghostly images
Shadows are its beauty
Thorns its better half
Pain considered normal
No worries, no cares, no fears
Low as the dirt, the wind mumbles
While passing by
A rose standing alone
Will the sun save me? It cries
Blinded by cycles of pest
Watered by unstable rains
Why was I given to this garden?
Why was my seed planted here?
My thorns, my pains, but so dear
I, myself a rose
Far but ever so near

You Are A Love Song

When you are near, I pause
Listening to your heart's desire
You are my 'press play and record'
Your beautiful lyrics calm my spirit
Rewinding as you reminisce
About how we first met
And as you fast forward
Building our future in your thoughts
I love how you stop and re-record
When trouble arrives
You are my high note, forever in tune
My love song

I Long for You

Loving and kind
Bitter and cold
When anger ignites
Tongue is bold
You are my child
A joy in my sight
Not distance from wrong
But distance from right
You shine like a candle
But darkened by the flame
Misguided by worldly obsessions
Your heart no shame
Free but imprisoned
By sins deadly touch
I await reaching, so long, so much
My love for you is endless
Miles can't carry it away
My heart for you is crying
As this pen and paper say
Your heart knows me
Your ears stand near
My love awaits so close, so dear
I love you, I know you
With beats that never end
I stand patiently knocking
Waiting to be let in

- Jesus

Delayed Flowers

Why cry?
You never cried when I was broken
Why visit me now?
When I called, you never came
You stand and reminisce about my life
Why don't you tell them I was your shadow?
Not even recognized by you in light
You stand over me and you weep
I can't hear you
Your cries are now worthless
Why grasp and kiss my lifeless skin?
You knew that you shattered my heart
A heart that cried daily for God to piece together
Finally the day has come
Where I'm being acknowledged
I've waited so long for this special day
But why did that day
Have to be my funeral?
So in my casket as I lay
All alone as I lived
Only to die of a broken heart
I'm with Jesus and
I've met his father
And yes
We have forgiven you

Under the Old Tree

Where we once gathered
Remembering the silent nights
Sharing the hugs
That we give year after year
The spiritual gifts we will forever hold
The memories that will always be told
Another year
Under the old tree

While I Was Living

I was laughing
But your laughter was suddenly silenced
I was comfortable
But at that moment heartache held you
You needed that day but I didn't
I was happy
But your smile was interrupted
I heard the sounds of peace
But you heard chaos
My body excelled that day
But yours gave out
I was praying at that time
And I knew you were also
I remember the day that I stayed
but you left with death

Self Portrait

Thank you for believing in me
Thank you for giving me permission to love
Thank you for your now peace and joy
That you no longer dismiss from the goodness
above
Thank you for caring
Thank you for your positive thoughts
Thank you for allowing me to finally see myself
And not the shameless negative self talk
Thank you for allowing forgiveness to reign
Thank you for the losses you've strongly held
Thank you for the wins you've gained
And the pain you've quietly shelved
Thank you for my inner beauty
And for the finishing touches
But more importantly for the spilled paint
And the hardened brushes

My Shadow

No worries, no stress
My image, my own
No cares, heart is stone
Flaws are hidden
My pest attached to my pain
My problems it can't obtain
Tears are dark
Mind is cold, confidence is strong
Silent breath is bold
Often lonely
Isn't afraid to dream
My shadow
I wished I could be

Neighbor

You knock and knock
But I can't let you in
My home is unclean
There's mountains of clutter from head to toe
I constantly stand in filth and dust
I hear you knocking
But I'm too ashamed to let you in
Why do you continue to knock?
Why don't you believe no one's home?
Aren't you tired?
You have stood there for so long
So I finally cleaned my cluttered home
And I answered my door
And there stood Jesus
Patiently waiting for me to let him in

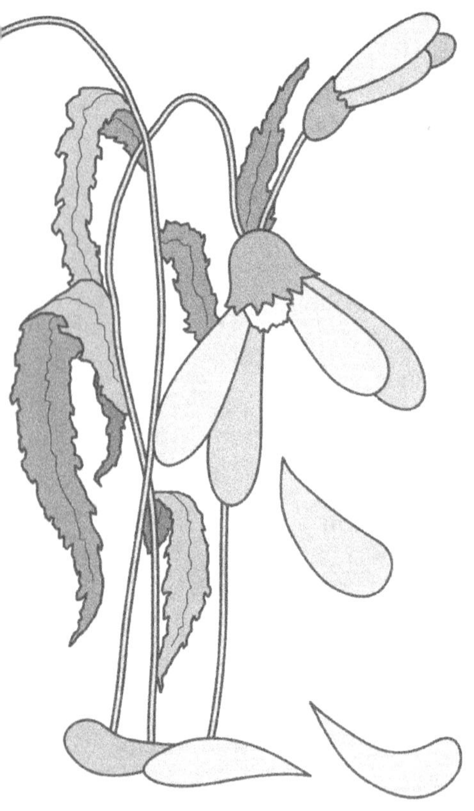

Wilted Weed

Standing there
Thyself is thy only
Waiting on the gardener to release thee
Swaying motionless
As the wind carries on
Am I my only?
Whispers the weed
Not given a name as elegant as the lily
Or as beautiful as the rose
Thy growth is thy curse, assumes the weed
Standing there, hopeless and willingly
Waiting on the gardener to release thee

Awaken Sunrise

Wake up, sunrise
Why do you sleep on my time?
I am no longer awakened by the sounds of the
rooster
Has the nightfall taken you hostage?
Is daybreak no longer your friend?
Has the sunset weakened your strength?
Why do you sleep on my time?
You are hidden behind the potters test
Given to strengthen my inner me
Joy is a daybreak away
Time is a constant battle
Don't let darkness take me captive
Awake sunrise
And rise upon me

My Soldier Overseas

Overseas, oh how I oversee
Your love away prospering for me
I race to the touch of your letters
As we comfort each other through the ink of our
pens
Alone and away
Two words that rest peacefully
But are at a constant war
Do not let the shore wash you to another
My soldier overseas
On how I oversee
Your love away prospering for me

Dear You,

You are more beautiful inside than out
An elegant flower with the scent of a rose
You are special with a heart of gold
Beautiful like the Grand Canyon - so deep
The twinkle in an eye
And the sun at its peak
You are a beautiful painting
That artists flock to see
The scenery of the calm ocean waves
Where everyone wants to be
You are the imprint of beauty
You are a rare, one of a kind
Red diamond

- L.M.

Author Biography

LaToya Martin was born and raised in the small town of Boley, Oklahoma. She is the mother of two teenage daughters. Writing was never her passion; she only began writing because of a few homework assignments. Over the years, however, her love for writing blossomed. Her poetry has been published in 3-4 different local magazines and newspapers. When she isn't writing, LaToya Martin loves fishing, visiting haunted locations, and photography.